CRIMINAL COP

KIRAN KUMAR R

Contents

Acknowledgements

I wish to express my gratitude to TEJASVNI.K who helped me in proof reading which made possible in preparation of the book.

Prologue

IN NORTH AMERICA.

NORTH AMERICA WAS A FAMOUS COUNTRY IN THE WORLD. CUBA IS A SMALL ISLAND SITUATED IN NORTH AMERICA. NORTH AMERICA HAD NOT GIVEN ANY IMPORTANCE TO THE PEOPLE IN CUBA. THE PEOPLE IN CUBA WERE HIGHLY DISCRIMINATED BY NORTH AMERICANS. CUBANS STARTED TO RISE THEIR VOICE AGAINST THIS DISCRIMINATION. THEY BUILT THEIR OWN GOVERNMENT IN SEARCH OF FREEDOM. BUT, NORTH AMERICA STARTED TO ATTACK THEM ECONOMICALLY BY STOPPING THE TRADE BETWEEN CUBA FROM ALL OTHER COUNTRIES. CUBANS SEARCHED A LEADER TO LEAD THEM IN A CORRECT PATH. THERE CAME FRIEDAL CASTRO. HE LEAD THE COUNTRY AND PEOPLE LIKE A GREAT LEADER. HE WAS READY TO SACRIFICE HIS LIFE FOR CUBA. HE TOOK A BIG DECISION TO MAKE THE NEEDS OF THEIR PEOPLE HIS OWN. HE DECIDED NOT TO DEPEND ON ANY COUNTRY FOR THEIR NEEDS AS FOR NOW. HE STRENGTHENED HIS ARMY, MEDICAL DEPARTMENT AND BECAME ONE OF TOP 5 RANKS IN ARMY AND 1ST RANK IN MEDICAL ALL OVER THE WORLD.CUBA BECAME INDEPENDENT AND DEMOCRATIC. ALL THESE THINGS WERE HAPPENED BECAUSE OF ONE MAN'S LEADERSHIP. THE NAME FRIEDAL CASTRO STARTED TO SPREAD ALL OVER THE WORLD. BECAUSE OF HIS BOLD DECISIONS AND FAITH ON HIMSELF, HE EARNED

MORE RESPECT AND CREATED A POWERFUL SOCIETY. HE MADE A HUGE HISTORY AND ONE DAY AS ALL HUMAN BEINGS, HIS LAST DAY ON EARTH ARRIVED AT THE AGE OF 60. HE DIED AS A PRESIDENT OF CUBA. HUGE CROWD ARRIVED FOR HIS FUNERAL AND DEATH CEREMONY. CUBA LOST THE BIG PILLAR OF THE COUNTRY.

AFTER SOMEDAYS,

PEOPLE OF CUBA CHOSE ALBERTO KORDA AS A PRESIDENT OF CUBA TO TAKE THE PLACE OF LEGEND FRIEDAL CASTRO. ALBERTO KORDA WAS GOOD HEARTED AND A RIGHT PERSON TO LEAD THE COUNTRY. HE HAD TWO CHILDREN, HIS DAUGHTER NAMED 'MARIO CIMMARO' AND HIS SON NAMED ' RAUL CORRALES'.

CHAPTER ONE

THE CASE

AT HAVANA (CAPITAL OF CUBA),

IN JOSE MARTI AIRPORT, A MAN WAS CHASING A WOMEN TO A ABONDED HOUSE AND LOCKED THE DOOR. THE INFORMATION REACHED THE COPS AND THEY ARRIVED AS SOON AS POSSIBLE. THOMAS SANCHER WAS THE COP WHO TOOK CHARGE ON THIS CASE. WHEN THE COPS WENT INSIDE THE HOUSE, THEY NOTICED THAT THE WOMEN HAD BEEN KILLED. THOMAS NOTICED A CHAIN IN HER HAND. HE TOOK THE CHAIN AND SEARCHED FOR MORE EVIDANCES. HE GOT ANOTHER EVIDENCE AS A CAR KEY WITH A SYMBOL OF GMC. HE SENT THE DEAD BODY TO MORTUARY. AND HE ALSO NOTICED THAT THE CHAIN DOLLAR HAD THE NAME "JAMES."

THE INVESTIGATION

THOMAS STARTED TO INVESTIGATE ABOUT THE CAR KEY IN ALL COMPANIES OVER HAVANA. IT WAS NOT USEFUL BECAUSE THE CAR COMPANY WHICH THE KEY BELONGS IS NOT THERE IN HAVANA. SO HE

STARTED TO SEARCH ALL OVER CUBA WITH THE HELP OF HIS FRIENDS, BUT ALL WENT IN WAIN. NO COMPANIES WERE ABLE TO IDENTIFY THE KEY. THEN, THOMAS GOT A CALL FROM HOSPITAL STATING THAT THE POST-MORTEM REPORT IS READY. THOMAS REACHED THE HOSPITAL. THERE HE MET FAIZON (FRIEND OF FRIEDAL CASTRO AND ONE OF THE MAIN REASON FOR CUBA'S INDEPENDENCE). THOMAS REALISED THAT THE WOMEN THAT GOT KILLED WAS FAIZON'S DAUGHTER. THOMAS MET DOCTOR AND ASKED ABOUT THE REPORT. DOCTOR STATED THAT THE GIRL HAD TAKEN HIGH DOSE OF DRUG BEFOE SHE WAS KILLED AND HE ALSO SAID THAT THE INTENSITY OF THE DRUG TOOK 50% OF HER LIFE BEFORE SHE HAVE BEEN KILLED. THOMAS ASKED ABOUT THE NAME OF DRUG. DOCTOR SAID THAT THE SAMPLE WAS GIVEN FOR RESEARCH.

THOMAS WAS THE HEAD COMMANDER OF COPS IN HAVANA. AS SAME AS THOMAS, STEVEN BAUER IS ONE OF THE HEAD COMMANDER WHO TOOK FLORIDA UNDER CONTROL. STEVEN BAUER IS ARROGENT BUT INTELLIGENT. STEVEN BAUR WAS CURRENTLY HANDLING THE CASE OF JOHN CREKIN'S SON'S DEATH. (JOHN CREKIN IS ALSO A FIGHTER WHO FOUGHT FOR INDEPENDENCE). JOHN CREKIN'S SON WAS A FAMOUS ACTOR SO A HUGE CROWD ARRIVED FOR HIS DEATH CEREMONY. DUE TO INSUFFUCIENT COPS FORCE THOMAS AND HIS TEAM WERE ASSINGNED DUTY IN FLORIDA. THERE THOMAS MET STEVEN AND INVESTIGATED ABOUT THE DEATH OF JOHN CREKIN'S SON. STEVEN SAID THAT HE TOOK A HIGH DOZE OF A DANGEROUS

DRUG WHICH AFFECTED HIS HEALTH IN 5 HOURS AND LEAD TO DEATH. THOMAS ASKED ABOUT THE DRUG. STEVEN SAID THE DRUG NAME WAS FLUNITRAZEPAM (ILLEGAL ROHYPNOL). THEN THOMAS HAD A CALL FROM HOSPITAL AND THEY SAID THE NAME OF DRUG USED BY THE WOMEN WAS "ROHYPNOL". FROM THIS THOMAS CAME TO KNOW THAT THE MURDER WAS ALREADY PLANNED. BECAUSE THE DEAD PERSONS ARE THE CHILDREN OF THE LEADERS AND THE DRUG USED IS OF SAME TYPE.

CUBA IS THE TOP MOST COUNTRY IN MEDICAL DEPARTMENT , DESPITR THAT THEY DO NOT CONSIDER ROHYPNOL DRUG FOR USAGE DUE TO ITS HARMFUL EFFECTS. THOMAS SHARED ABOUT THE CASE WITH STEVEN. THEN STEVEN AND THOMAS STARTED TO WORK TOGETHER TO FIND THE PERSON OR A GROUP BEHIND THIS CRIME.

THOMAS SANCHER AND STEVEN BAUER

THOMAS AND STEVEN TOGETHER STARTED TO INVESTIGATE ABOUT THE CASE. AN ASST POLICE OF THOMAS MADE A CALL STATING THAT HE SAW A MAN WITH GUN INSIDE A SUPERMARKET AND HE WAS WEARING A FACE MASK WHEN MOVING OUT. THOMAS ORDERED HIM TO FOLLOW THE UNKNOWN MAN. THE ASST COP STARTED FOLLOWING HIM. HE MOVED TO SANTA CLARA. THE COP, ALDO FOLLOWED HIM. WHEN THE MAN WENT INSIDE THE HOME, THE COP TOOK THE PHONE AND CALLED THOMAS, HE STARTED " HE IS THE ..." , AND THERE WAS NO SOUND AFTER THESE WORDS. THOMAS SENSED SOMETHING IS WRONG. SO THOMAS

PLANNED TO GO TO SANTA CLARA. AT THAT TIME ALBERTO KORDA CALLED HIM TO HIS HOME. SO THOMAS MADE STEVEN TO MOVE TO SANTA CLARA AND HE WENT TO KORDA'S HOME. THERE KORDA SAID THOMAS TO INCREASE THE SECURITY AROUND HIS HOME FOR A PROTECTION FOR HIS CHILDREN. THOMAS AGREED AND STARTED TO MOVE. THAT TIME KORDA'S DAUGHTER MARIO CIMMARO ASKED THOMAS TO EAT CHOCOLATE WHICH IS OF NEW BRAND. THOMAS , WHO WAS TENSED ABOUT THE CASE , DECLINED KINDLY AND LEFT THE HOME. HE MOVED TO SANTA CLARA. THERE HE SAW THE COP WAS SHOT AND HE DEAD. THOMAS WENT INSIDE THE HOME OF THE UNKNOWN MAN TO GATHER EVIDANCES. THERE STEVEN GAVE A KEYCHAIN NAMED TRIC. THOMAS NOTICED THERE ARE MANY CHOCOLATE WRAPPERS ON THE FLOOR. HE TOOK ONE OF THEM AND A SUDDEN REALISATION HIT HIM, THAT WAS THE SAME CHOCOLATE THAT WAS IN THE HANDS OF MARIO CIMMARO. HE IMMEDIATELY CALLED ALBERTO TO ALERT HIM. BUT UNFORTUNATELY THERE , MARIO CIMMARO WAS ALREADY DEAD BECAUSE OF THE DRUG PRESENT IN THE CHOCOLATE. THE DRUG WAS ARTIFICIALLY INSERTED INTO THE CHOCOLATE. THE DAUGHTER OF ANOTHER LEADER HAVE BEEN KILLED.

THOMAS WAS CONFUSED AND DEVASTATED . HE WENT TO HIS OFFICE (POLICE STATION). HE TOOK ALL THE EVIDENCES AND KEPT ON A TABLE. HE HAS A DOLLAR WITH NAME JAMES, A CAR KEY WITH NAME GMC, A KEYCHAIN WITH NAME TRIC, A DRUG ROHYPNOL AND CHOCOLATE WRAPPERS. HE NOTICED A CRACK ON THE DOLLAR AT THE LAST

LETTER OF JAMES AND A CRACK ON THE KEYCHAIN AT FIRST LETTER OF TRIC. HE JOINED THE DOLLAR AND FOUND THAT THEY ARE PERFECTLY MATCHED. (FAIZON'S DAUGHTER BROKE THE DOLLAR BEFORE SHE HAD BEEN KILLED SO THE KILLER HAD THE REMAINING PART TRIC). THEN HE UNDERSTOOD THAT THE KILLER'S NAME WAS "JAMES TRIC". THE CHOCOLATE NAME WRITTEN IN THE WRAPPER WAS HEILMANN CHOCOLATES. AT THE BACK OF THE WRAPPER IT WAS WRITTEN THAT IT WAS MADE IN GERMANY, MUNICH. THERE STEVEN CAME AND SAID THAT HE FOUND THE NAME OF CAR COMPANY AND THE PLACE WHERE DRUG IS PRODUCED. THOMAS ASKED ABOUT THE CAR COMPANY. STEVEN SAID THAT IT WAS 'GERMAN MOTOR COMPANY' AND SAID THAT THE ILLEGAL ROHYPNOL DRUG IS FROM SWEDEN. (THE ORIGINAL ROHYPNOL GIVEN TO THEM WAS AVAILABLE ONLY IN SWEDEN). BUT HE WAS CONFUSED HOW THE KILLER HAD LINKED WITH SWEDEN TO GET THE DRUGS. SO, THOMAS MADE A CALL TO HIS POLICE FRIEND ADOLF (HEAD POLICE IN GERMANY) AND ASKED HIM HELP FOR THE INVESTIGATION. NOW THOMAS AND STEVEN WERE READY TO GO TO GERMANY.

CHAPTER TWO

INVESTIGATION AT GERMANY

AT GERMANY,

IN BERLIN AIRPORT. ADOLF ARRANGED A ROOM AND TAXI FOR HIS FRIEND THOMAS SANCHER WHO COMES TO GERMANY FOR AN INVESTIGATION. AFTER THE ARRIVAL OF THOMAS, ADOLF WENT TO HELP HIM WITH THE INVESTIGATION. THERE STEVEN EXPLAINED ABOUT THE CASE. THOMAS BROUGHT ALL THE EVIDENCES AND SHOWED IT TO ADOLF. ADOLF SAW THE CHOCOLATE WRAPPER AND FOUND THAT IT WAS MADE IN MUNICH. SO ON THE NEXT DAY HE TOOK THOMAS AND STEVEN TO THE HEILEMANN CHOCOLATE COMPANY, MUNICH. THERE THEY MET THE COMPANY MANAGER ,MR.PETER HUBER. ADOLF ASKED ABOUT THE TRADE OF CHOCOLATES OVER OTHER COUNTRIES. PETER STATED THAT THE CHOCOLATES WERE TRADED TO VARIOUS COUNTRIES BUT MOSTLY THE ORIGINAL

BRAND IS AVAILABLE IN GERMANY. THEN THOMAS SHOWED THE WRAPPER AND ASKED ABOUT IT. PETER SAID THAT IT SEEMED TO BE THE ORIGINAL BRAND. THEN THEY MOVED TO POTSDAM WHERE THE GERMAN MOTOR COMPANY IS PRESENT. THERE THEY MET THE GMC MANAGER ,ANNA HUBERIN. THOMAS SHOWED THE CAR KEY AND INVESTIGATED ABOUT IT. ANNA SAID THAT THE KEY BELONGED TO THE GMC COMPANY. ANNA QUESTIONED ABOUT THE INVESTIGATION TO ADOLF. ADOLF SAID THAT THOMAS AND STEVEN ARE HIS FRIENDS FROM CUBA CAME HERE FOR AN INVESTIGATION. THEN ANNA SAID THAT THE CAR WAS EXCLUSIVELY MADE FOR GERMAN PEOPLE AND ITS NOT BEING TRADED TO ANY COUNTRY. THIS STATEMENT MADE THOMAS TO CONFIRM THAT JAMES TRIC WAS GERMAN. WHEN ADOLF, THOMAS AND STEVEN MOVED OUT OF THE COMPANY, ANNA MADE A CALL TO HER UNCLE AND SAID HIM ABOUT THE INVESTIGATION. (ANNA'S UNCLE IS NONE OTHER THAN PETER HUBER). HE SAID THAT THEY ALREADY INVESTIGATED ABOUT THE CHOCOLATE. AFTER THE INVESTIGATION THOMAS GONE TO HIS ROOM AND STARTED TO READ BOOKS (HISTORY OF GERMANY). HE SAW THE KEYCHAIN/DOLLAR (WITH NAME JAMESTRIC) ON THE TABLE. HE CLOSELY WATCHED THE DOLLAR AND FOUND A SMALL WORD WAS WRITTEN ON THE DOLLAR. HE NOTICED THAT THE WORD WAS "SWED" THE REMAINING LETTERS ON THE WORDS WAS MISSING. THOMAS SHOWED THE DOLLAR TO ADOLF AND ASKED ABOUT THE MATERIAL BY WHICH THE DOLLAR IS MADE UP OF. ADOLF REPLIED THAT THE MATERIAL WAS IRON. SUDDENLY, THOMAS TOOK

THE BOOK AND STARTED TO READ THE PAGE FROM FIRST. THERE HE FOUND THAT THE MAXIMUM AMOUNT OF MINARAL ORE ARE EXPORTED FROM GERMANY TO SWEDEN. EXSPECIALLY THE IRON ORE ARE EXPORTED TO SWEDEN IRON INDUSTRIES WHERE THE IRON BASED MATERIALS ARE MANUFACTURED. FROM THESE INFORMATION THOMAS FOUND THAT THE WORD WRITTEN ON THE DOLLAR WAS 'SWEDEN' AND IT WAS MADE IN SWEDEN. STEVEN AND THOMAS SPEND 6 DAYS IN GERMANY FOR THEIR INVESTIGATION. ONE EVENING, THEY WERE WALKING TOWARDS IRON ORE MINING CENTRE, HAMBURG, GERMANY. HAMBURG IS AN INDUSTRIAL PLACE WHERE POPULATION WAS LESS AS COMPARED TO OTHER STATES. ON THAT SILENT EVENING A BIKE WITH A FIREY EXHAUSTER SOUND CROSSED THEM WITH A HIGH SPEED. A MAN SITTING AT THE BACK SHOT WITH A GUN. ADOLF AND THOMAS TOOK THEIR GUN AND STARTED TO SHOOT. BUT THE RIDER WAS RIDING THE BIKE IN A ZIG ZAG MANNER WHICH IS UNCOMFORTABLE TO SHOOT. THERE THOMAS SHOT THE PERSON SITTING AT THE BACK. HE SHOT HIM AT HIS SHOULDER. THE PERSON FELLDOWN FROM THE BIKE AND THE RIDER ESCAPED FROM THERE. THOMAS GONE NEAR THE UNKNOWN PERSON AND REMOVED THE MASK. THERE ADOLF CALLED THOMAS AND SAID THAT STEVEN HAS BEEN SHOT DEAD BY THAT PERSON. WHEN THOMAS TURN TOWARDS THE PERSON, HE NOTICED THAT IT WAS ANNA HUBERIN (GMC MANAGER). SHE HAD A GUN IN HER HAND. SHE LAUGHED AND SHOT HERSELF. NOW THOMAS LOST HIS INVESTIGATOR FRIEND STEVEN

AND A HUGE EVIDANCE ANNA. HE CONVEYED THE MESSAGE TO STEVEN FAMILY AND CUBAN PEOPLE. THOMAS GOT THE NEWS THAT CUBA WAS ATTACKED WITH 2 BOMB BLAST AND GUN SHOOTINGS. CUBAN GOVERNMENT ORDERED LOCKDOWN FOR THE PEOPLE'S SAFETY. ADOLF BROUGHT THE BULLET WHICH HITS STEVEN AND GAVE TO THOMAS. THOMAS NOTED THE BULLET WAS FAMILIAR TO HIM. HE TOOK HIS PHONE AND SEARCHED THE IMAGE OF HIS ASST POLICE DEATH (THE POLICE WHO HAS BEEN SHOT AT SANTA CLARA BY JAMES). THERE HE FOUND THAT THE BULLET USED BY JAMES AND ANNA WAS THE SAME.

THOMAS AND GERMAN PRESIDENT

AT ADOLF'S OFFICE. ADOLF SAID THAT HE CAN'T BE WITH THOMAS ON THAT DAY DUE TO HIS BUSY SCHEDULE OF PROTECTING PRESIDENT. THOMAS REQUSTED TO JOIN WITH ADOLF IN THIS PROTECTION DUTY. ADOLF ACCEPTED AND THE GONE TO DRESDEN, GERMANY. THERE PRESIDENT ARRIVED. HE STARTED TO GIVE A SPEECH ON THE STAGE. THE CROWD WAS HUGE. THOMAS INFORMED THE POSITION OF EACH PERSON WHO SEEMS TO BE DOUBTFUL TO ADOLF. ADOLF AND HIS TEAM FOLLOWED THE INSTRUCTIONS SAID BY THOMAS. EACH TEAM MEMBER FOCUSED ON EACH PERSON WHO SEEMS TO BE DOUBTFUL. THE PERSONS

STARTED TO MOVE TOWARDS THE PRESIDENT. SUDDENLY, AN UNKNOWN VOICE SAID TO SHOOT. THEN THE DOUBTED PERSONS TOOK THEIR GUN, LOADED AND POINTED TOWARDS PRESIDENT. ALL OF THE SUDDEN, THE COPS SURROWNDED THEM AND SAVED PRESIDENT. THE OPERATION BECOMES SUCESSFULL AND PRRSIDENT SAVED BECAUSE OF THOMAS. SO ADOLF INTRODUCED THOMAS AND EXPLAINED ABOUT THE INVESTIGATION. GERMAN PRESIDENT PROMISED THAT HE WILL BE SUPPORTIVE FOR HIS CASE. AFTER THESE HARD DAYS IN GERMANY, THOMAS MOVES TO CUBA.

AT CUBA,

THE STREETS OF CUBA WERE EMPTY. THOMAS MET ALBERTO KORDA AND HAD A MEETING ABOUT THE LOCKDOWN. KORDA SAID THAT LOCKDOWN IS THE SAFEST WAY TO PROTECT PEOPLE FROM ATTACK BECAUSE THE MILITARY BASE IS ALSO BLASTED AND MANY EQUIPMENTS ARE DAMAGED.THOMAS REQUSTED TO CANCEL THE ORDER AND LET THE PEOPLE IN STREETS FOR THEIR NORMAL LIFE. THOMAS ARRANGED HIS POLICE TEAM TO GUARD PEOPLES ALLOVER THE STREETS. KORDA QUESTIONED ABOUT THE INVESTIGATION. THOMAS REPLIED THAT HE WAS NEAR TO THE CRIMINAL BUT FOR FURTHER DETAILS HE NEEDS TO MOVE TOWARDS SWEDEN. THEN THOMAS STARTED HIS JOURNEY TO SWEDEN.

CHAPTER THREE

MOVING TO SWEDEN

AT SWEDEN,

THOMAS REACHED SWEDEN. ON THE NEXT DAY, HE MET OLIVER (POLICE HIGHER OFFICIAL IN SWEDEN). THOMAS SHOWED HIS POLICE ID PROOF TO OLIVER AND ASKED FOR HELP. THEY STARTED THEIR INVESTIGATION FROM THE IRON MANUFACTURING INDUSTRY AT MALMO, SWEDEN. OLIVER STATED THAT THIS WAS THE WELLKNOWN INDUSTRY FOR PRODUCING THE STATIONARIES. THERE THEY MET WILLIAM (MANAGER IN IRON MANUFACTURING INDUSTRIES). THEN, OLIVER SHOWED THE MANAGER HIS ID PROOF AND INVESTIGATED ABOUT THE DOLLAR. WILLIAM THEN CONFIRMED THAT THE DOLLAR WAS MADE THERE. SECONDLY, THEY WENT TO THE PLACE WHERE ILLEGAL DRUGS ARE PRODUCED. THEY DISGUISED AS DRUG ADDICTS IN NEED OF DRUGS.

THE SECURITY WAS TIGHT BUT DESPITE THAT NO ONE DOUBTED THEM .INSIDE THE PLACE THEY MET OSCAR (ONE OF THE DRUG DEALER) AND BROUGHT

DRUGS. USING THIS SITUATION, THEY STARTED TO INVESTIGATE ABOUT ROHYPNOL DRUG. THERE THEY CAME TO KNOW THAT THE DRUG WAS PRODUCED AND TRADED TO OTHER COUNTRIES BUT THE HEAVY DOSE WITH HARMFULL EFFECT IS AVAILABLE ONY IN SWEDEN. THE INVESTIGATION TOOK 3 DAYS. HE GOT SOME IDEAS FROM THE INVESTIGATION DONE UPTO THE DATE.

THOMAS SANCHER AND JAMES TRIC

AFTER THESE INVESTIGATION. THOMAS LEFT TO HIS ROOM TO TAKE REST. THERE HE SAW A LETTER ON THE TABLE. HE TOOK IT AND READ. THE LETTER SAID, " HI, I AM JAMESTRIC. I CAME TO KNOW THAT YOU ARE DEALING THE CASE. PLEASE GET AWAY FROM MY WAY. I'VE LOST MY SISTER (ANNA) BECAUSE OF YOU AND EARLIER I'VE LOST MY FAMILY BECAUSE OF YOUR COUNTRY. SO DON'T CROSS IN MY WAY. THIS IS A STATEMENT THAT, THE PERSONS INTERFERING ON MY WAY HAVE TO MEET DEATH SOON. THE REPLY LETTER CAN BE WRITTEN AND PLEASE KEEP IT ON THE SHOE RACK OF ROOM NO:701". THOMAS WROTE A REPLY LETTER AND KEPT THAT ON THE RACK AS ASKED. HE WALKED SLOWLY TOWARDS HIS ROOM. AT HIS BACK, THE ELEVETOR DOOR OPENS. A MAN WITH MASK AND GLOVES TOOK THE LETTER AND CLOSED THE DOOR. THOMAS STARTED TO RUN DOWN THE STAIRCASE. HE GOT DOWN .THERE HE SAW JAMES TAKING A BIKE TO ESCAPE. FORTUNATELY OLIVER CAME THERE AT THE RIGHT TIME. THOMAS TOLD HIM TO SIT BEHIND AND HE STARTED TO DRIVE THE BIKE. JAMES WAS

HEADING TOWARDS GOTHENBURG. THOMAS CHASING JAMES IN THE MALMO - GOTHENBURG HIGHWAY. OLIVER ALERTED THE COPS AND A POLICE CAR JOINED THE CHASE. AT A RAILWAY CROSSING, THE GATE WAS CLOSED. JAMES TURNED THE BIKE AND STARTED TO MOVE ALONG THE WAY OF TRAIN. BUT, THE POLICE CAR CANT ABLE TO MAKE A SHARP TURN. SO THE CAR MET WITH AN ACCIDENT. THOMAS TURNED HIS BIKE AND CONTINUED THE CHASE. SUDDENLY, A MAN INSIDE THE TRAIN SHOT ON THOMAS'S HAND. HE LEFT THE BIKE AND FELL DOWN. THOMAS NOTICED THAT THE SHOOTER WAS PETER HUBER (MANAGER OF HEILLMANN CHOCOLATE COMPANY). THOMAS AND OLIVER WERE ADMITTED IN HOSPITAL. THE NEXT DAY, ADOLF ARRIVED TO SWEDEN AFTER HEARING THE NEWS OF THOMAS ACCIDENT. THERE THOMAS EXPLAINED ABOUT THE INVESTIGATION IN SWEDEN AND SAID THAT THE SHOOTER WAS PETER HUBER. ADOLF ALSO BROUGHT A INFORMATION THAT, IMAGE OF THE BULLET GIVEN TO HIM BY THOMAS BELONGED TO NORTH AMERICA.

AT JAMES HOME,

PETER HUBER AND JAMES WERE DISCUSSING ABOUT THE PLAN. THERE JAMES TOOK THE REPLY LETTER FROM THOMAS AND STARTED TO READ. THE REPLY BY THOMAS CONTAINS " HI JAMES, THIS IS THOMAS. IF YOU ARE READY TO TAKE RISKS FOR THE REVENGE ON MY COUNTRY DUE TO YOUR LOST FAMILY. THEN I AM READY TO TAKE RISK TO MEET THE DEATH".

AFTER READING THE LETTER JAMES CRUSHED IT AND THROWN INTO THE FIRE.

AFTER THE MEDICAL TREATMENT, THOMAS MOVED TO CUBA FOR SMALL INVESTIGATION. THERE, AGAIN HE SAW THE STREETS AND COLONIES WERE EMPTY IN FLORIDA SO HE MADE A CALL TO KORDA AND ASKED ABOUT IT. KORDA SAID THOMAS TO REACH HAVANA. WHEN THOMAS REACHED HAVANA, HE SAW ALL PEOPLES ARE HEADING TOWARDS THE BIG GROUND OF CUBA WHERE RAUL CORRALES (SON OF ALBERTO KORDA) WAS KILLED AND TIED ON THE POST. THOMAS WAS ASHAMED THAT HE COULDN'T SAVE ANOTHER LEADER'S CHILD, BUT HE HAD HOPES AND SINCE HE WAS VERY CLOSE TO CATCHING THE CRIMINAL, HE WILL SOMEDAY SUCCED ON IT. THE DEATH CEREMONY WAS ARRANGED AND DONE. AFTER SOMEDAYS, A POLICEAN STARTED TO BEHAVE ABNORMALLY. HE STARTED TO SHOOT PUBLIC. BUT OTHER POLICE OFFICERS SAVED THEM. THOMAS GOT AN INFORMATION THAT MANY PEOPLES IN CUBA STARTED TO BEHAVE ABNORMALLY. SO HE ARRANGED A MEDICAL TEAM TO RESEARCH ON THIS. THE DOCTORS SAID THAT THE FOOD TOOK BY THE PATIENTS ARE FILLED WITH ROHYPNOL. EXPECIALLY THE FOOD ITEMS WHICH IS MADE AND PRODUCED BY OUR OWN COUNTRY CUBA. MANY PEOPLE ARE AFFECTED BY THIS FOOD INCLUDING DOCTORS. SO, HE ARRANGED PROFFESIONAL DOCTORS FROM SWEDEN TO TREAT PEOPLE OF CUBA. HE ARRANGED THE DOCTOR TEAM WITH HELP OF OLIVER. OLIVER SENT 2 PROFFESIONAL DOCTORS (LIAM AND ELIAS TUANAH) TO CUBA. THEIR DUTY WAS IN GOVERNMENT HOSPITAL OF CUBA. AFTER

THESE ARRANGEMENTS, THOMAS WENT TO KORDA'S HOME. THERE HE CAME TO KNOW THAT KORDA IS ALSO AFFECTED BY THIS DRUG. SO, THOMAS ARRANGED A SPECIAL TREATMENT FOR KORDA. THE SITUATION AT CUBA BECAME WORSE. THE PEOPLE STARTED TO PROTEST AGAIST THE GOVERNMENT. PRESIDENT IS UNDER MEDICAL TREATMENT. THE GOVERNMENT OF CUBA STARTED TO FALL. AS THERE IS NO OTHER GO, THOMAS ATTENDED THE PROTEST MEETING IN FLORIDA INSTEAD OF PRESIDENT. THOMAS EXPLAINED THE PROBLEM TO THE PEOPLE. PEOPLE STARTED TO IGNORE THE SPEECH AND DEMANDED THAT, THEY NEEDED A POWERFUL GOBERNMENT. THERE A POLICE OFFICER WHO IS VERY CLOSE TO THOMAS COULDN'T SEE THOMAS AT THIS SITUATION. HE HAS A GREAT RESPECT ON THOMAS AND HIS DEDICATION TOWARDS COUNTRY. SO HE GOT THE MIC FROM THOMAS AND SAID THAT IF THE GOVERNMENT OF CUBA UNDER MR.ALBERTO KORDA IS NOT GOOD, THOMAS WILL BE ANNOUNCED AS A NEW PRESIDENT. THE CROUD STOPPED THEIR CHAOS AND THE PLACE BECAME SILENT.

CHAPTER FOUR

HISTORY AND MISTERY

ON THE NEXT DAY 12.00 AM, ALBERTO KORDA DIED EVEN AFTER A SPECIAL MEDICAL TREATMENT. THE PEOPLE OF CUBA FELT SAD FOR HIS DEATH. HE WAS A GREAT LEADER BUT THE SITUATION AND PRESSURE MADE HIM TAKE SOME WRONG DECISIONS. THE CUBAN GOVERNMENT HAD TOTALLY FALLEN. MANY HIGHER OFFICIALS HAD A MEETING TO REBUILD THE GOVERNMENT STRONGER. THEY ASKED THOMAS TO LEAD THE COUNTRY BY SEEING HIS DEDICATION TOWARDS COUNTRY. BUT THOMAS DECLINED AND SAID THAT THE PRESIDENT POSITION HAD HUGE RESPONSIBLITIES, PRESSURE AND HE STATED THAT HE NEEDS TO FINISH HIS INVESTIGATION ON THIS CASE WHICH NEEDS A FREE MIND TO FOCUS. THEN THEY SELECTED FAIZON AS THE NEW PRESIDENT OF CUBA. ANNOUNCEMENT WAS MADE TO THE PEOPLE THAT, TEMPORARILY BY ANALYZING THE SITUATION FAIZON IS APPOINTED AS THE PRESIDENT, AFTER THE SITUATION BECOMES NORMAL PEOPLE CAN SELECT THEIR OWN LEADER BY HAVING AN ELECTION. ON THE NEXT DAY FAIZON

GOT THE POWER IN HIS HANDS TO LEAD THE COUNTRY. THOMAS MET FAIZON FOR AN INVESTIGATION. THOMAS ASKED ABOUT THE HISTORY OF CONNECTION BETWEEN CUBA AND SWEDEN. FAIZON REPLIED THAT THERE WERE ONLY SMALL TRADE DONE BETWEEN SWEDEN AND CUBA. THERE IS NO OTHER RELATION. THEN THOMAS ASKED ABOUT THE RELATION BETWEEN GERMANY AND CUBA.

GERMANY, CUBA AND JAMESTRIC

HE SAID THAT GERMANY AND NORTH AMERICA WERE ENIMIES AT THAT TIME. THE BOMBS FROM NORTH AMERICA DAMAGED MOST OF THE PLACES IN GERMANY. FURTHER FOR REVENGE, GERMANY STARTED TO BLAST BOMBS ON NORTH AMERICA. BUT THE FIGHT DID NOT LAST LONG. THEY STARTED TO UNDERSTAND EACHOTHER AND STARTED TRADING AND EXPORTING THINGS. THE FRIENDSHIP BETWEEN THEM GREW FOR A LONG TIME. BUT THE PEOPLE OF NORTH AMERICA DIDN'T LIKE THE PEOPLE OF GERMANY. THEY STARTED TO DISCRIMINATE THE GERMANS WHO CAME TO NORTH AMERICA IN SEARCH FOR A LIVING BECAUSE OF HITLER'S HARSH RULING IN GERMANY. KURK AND HIS FAMILY IS ONE OF THEM WHO CAME TO NORTH AMERICA. BUT DUE TO DISCRIMINATION, THEY ARRIVED TO CUBA. KURK'S FAMILY INCLUDED 4 PERSONS. KURK HIMSELF, HIS WIFE MANSON AND THEIR SON AND DAUGHTER. WHEN THEY ARRIVED TO CUBA, THE PEOPLE OF CUBA HAD A BAD OPINION ON NORTH AMERICANS. KURK'S FAMILY WAS ALSO

FROM NORTH AMERICA. SO THE PEOPLE OF CUBA STARTED TO TORTURE KURK FAMILY BY THROWING STONES AT THEIR HOME. ONE DAY, WHEN KURK'S CHILDREN WENT TO THE MARKET FOR PURCHASING VEGETABLES, SOME CUBANS AGAIN STARTED TO DISTURB KURK. WHEN KURK RAISED HIS VOICE AGAINST THEM, THEY KILLED KURK AND MANSON. THEN THE NOTICE CAME FROM GERMANY THAT THE KURK FAMILY BELONGED TO GERMANY AND A CASE HAD BEEN FILED IN GERMANY STATING THAT KURK AND HIS FAMILY WAS MISSING. THOMAS ASKED ABOUT THE CHILDREN. FAIZON SAID THAT THE NAME OF THE BOY WAS JAMES AND THE GIRL , ANNA. THOMAS WAS SHOCKED AND ASKED," IS THE FULL NAME OF THE BOY JAMESTRIC?". FAIZON WAS CONFUSED ON HOW, HE KNEW THEIR NAMES AND ANSWERED,"YES". NOW THOMAS HAD A CLEAR IDEA ON JAMES AND HIS BACKGROUND. AFTER THE LONG CONVERSATION, THEY VISITED HOSPITALS TO CHECK THE CONDITION OF PATIENTS.

THE BLACK SHEEP

AT HOSPITAL, THOMAS SAW THAT MANY PEOPLE ARE IN SERIOUS CONDITION AND NO IMPROVEMENT HAS BEEN SEEN.THOMAS HEARD SOMEONE ARGUING INSIDE THE DOCTOR'S CABIN. THERE LIAM AND ELIAS WERE HAVING A COVERSATION ABOUT SOME UNKNOWN MAN. THE CONVERSATION WAS THAT IF THEY HELP THESE PEOPLE THEY WILL NOT GET BENEFITED BUT IF THE LEFT THEM AS IT IS TO DEATH, THE UNKNOWN MAN WILL PAY LIAM FAIRLY AND HE WILL GET BENIFITED. THOMAS OVERHEARD

THE ENTIRE CONVERSATION. WHEN LIAM OPENED THE DOOR, THERE THOMAS SAT ON THE CHAIR AND SAIS "GO AHEAD, KILL THE PEOPLE , AFTER ALL THATS WHAT WE ARE HERE FOR". LIAM AND ELIAS UNDERSTOOD THAT THOMAS HEARD THE CONVERSATION. SO LIAM PULLED THOMAS'S LEG AND ELIAS KICKED HIM. LIAM AND ELIAS RAN TO ESCAPE. BUT THOMAS ALERTED THE COPS AND ARRESTED LIAM AND ELIAS. AT POLICE STATION, THOMAS INVESTIGATED ABOUT THE UNKNOWN MAN WHO SAID THEM TO KILL THE PEOPLE. LIAM AND ELIAS WERE VERY ADAMENT. THEY WERE NOT ANSWERING ANY QUESTIONS. THEN, THOMAS STARTED TO TREAT THEM HARSHLY. ELIAS COULDN'T WITHSTAND THE TORTURE BY THOMAS SO SHE STARTED TO SAY THE TRUTH THAT, JAMESTRIC WAS WAS A DEAREST FRIEND OF ELIAS AND LIAM. AFTER LOSING HIS FAMILY, JAMES AND ANNA WENT TO SWEDEN IN SEARCH FOR THEIR LIVELYHOOD. JAMES WORKED IN A IRON MANUFACTURING COMPANY. HE WAS BRILLIANT IN MAKING KEYCHAIN, DOLLARS AND MANY IRON BASED MATERIALS. ONE DAY THE MELTED IRON MADE A INJURY ON HIS HAND. HE WAS ADMITTED IN LIAM'S HOSPITAL FOR TREATMENT. THERE JAMES SAID ABOUT HIS FAMILY AND SITUATION TO LIAM AND ELIAS. AFTER HEARING HIS SAD STORY LIAM AND ELIAS PROMISED HIM THAT THEY WILL HELP FOR JAMES AT ANY CAUSE. AFTER SOME YEARS, JAMES ASKED HELP FROM LIAM AND ELIAS AND SAID THAT THEY WILL ALSO BE PAID WITH A HUGE AMOUNT. AFTER THIS CONFESSIONS ,THOMAS REALISED THAT HE MISSED SOMETHING IN SWEDEN.

SO HE AGAIN PLANNED TO MOVE TO SWEDEN FOR INVESTIGATION.

AT SWEDEN,

THOMAS MET OLIVER AND EXPLAINED ABOUT THE EVIDENCES. OLIVER TOOK THOMAS TO THE MALMO IRON INDUSTRIES AND MET WILLIAM. THOMAS INVESTIGATED ABOUT JAMESTRIC. WILLIAM SAID THAT HE QUITED HIS JOB BEFORE 2 YEARS. THOMAS ASKED HIS PERSONNEL INFORMATION LIKE PHOTO AND PHONE NUMBER. WILLIAM GAVE JAMES PHOTO AND PHONE NUMBER. THEN THOMAS FORWARDED THE PHOTO AND NUMBER TO ALL HIS FRIENDS IN ALL COUNTRY AND SAID TO TRACK HIM. AFTER 2 DAYS, THOMAS GOT THE NEWS THAT JAMES WAS LOCATED IN CONCUN, NORTH AMERICA.

CHAPTER FIVE

THE TRUTH

AT CUBA,

THOMAS VISITED ALL PLACES IN HAVANA. HE NOTICED THAT THE CONDITION OF THE PEOPLE WERE BETTER. MANY OF THEM WERE DISCHARGED FROM HOSPITALS. AFTER SOMETIME, THOMAS HAD A CALL FROM UNKNOWN NUMBER. THOMAS ATTENDED THE CALL. IT WAS JAMES, HE SAID THAT HE WAS NOT EXPECTED THIS EFFORT FROM THOMAS BECAUSE THOMAS TRACED JAMES. JAMES ALSO ADDED THAT THE NEXT LEADER IS ALSO GOING TO MEET DEATH JUST LIKE ALBERTO KORDA. IF THOMAS WANTS TO SAVE THAT LEADER JAMES COMMANDED HIM TO GO TO THE JESSTER HOTEL IN FLORIDA. AFTER THESE WORDS, JAMES DISCONNECTED THE CALL. THOMAS DECIDED TO FACE THE RISK AND WENT TO THE JESSTER HOTEL. THERE HE GOT A LETTER FROM THE RECEPTIONIST WHICH INSTRUCTED HIM TO SAVE JOHN CREKINS. AFTER GETTING THIS INFORMATION THOMAS WENT TO JOHN'S HOME. THERE JOHN WAS SAFE. THOMAS WAS

COMFUSED. THEN HE GOT A CALL FROM THE SAME NUMBER. THERE, JAMES SAID THAT " HEY THOMAS, I THOUGHT YOU ARE A BRILLIANT COP. BUT, YOU COULDN'T EVEN ABLE TO GUESS THE LEADER. YOU ARE JUST FOLLOWING MY COMMANDS" AND LAUGHED. THEN THOMAS ASKED THAT WHO IS THE LEADER. JAMES REPLIED, IT WAS THE PRESIDENT FAIZON AND CUBA IS GOING TO LOSE THE 2ND PRESIDENT OF THE YEAR. THEN THOMAS STARTED TO LAUGH AND SAID JAMES TO MAKE A CALL TO HIS TEAM WHO GONE TO FAIZON'S HOME. JAMES FRIGHTENED. HE SUDDENLY MADE A CALL TO HIS TEAM. THERE THE PHONE WAS ATTENDED BY THE ASST POLICE OFFICER ROGER. ROGER GAVE THE PHONE TO JAMES TEAM LEADER. THE TEAM LEADER SAID THAT WHEN THEY CAME AND SURROUNDED FAIZON, THE POLICE TEAM POINTED THE GUN TOWARDS THEM. JAMES WAS SHOKED ,ASKED IF THERE WAS ANY WAY TO ESCAPE. THE TEAM LEADER REPLIED THAT THERE IS NO WAY EXEPT TO ATTACK THE COPS. THEN JAMES COMMANDED THEM TO DO SO. SUDDENLY THE TEAM MEMBERS STARTED TO SHOOT. THE POLICE ALSO STARTED TO SHOOT IN RESPONSE. THEIR TEAM CONSISTED OF 8 MEMBERS. THEY KILLED 3 COPS. THE COPS KILLED 5 OF THEM AND 3 GOT SHOT ON THEIR LEGS. WHEN THE POLICE WENT NEAR TO ARREST THEM. THEY SHOT THEMSELVES WITHOUT ANY DELAY. AGAIN THOMAS SANCHER LOST A HUGE EVIDANCE. THOMAS ARRIVED TO FAIZON'S HOME. THERE ROGER SAID THAT THE TEAM MEMBERS OF JAMES ARE MOST WANTED CRIMINALS IN NORTH AMERICA.

CUBA, NORTH AMERICA AND THOMAS

FROM THIS EVIDANCES, THOMAS CAME TO KNOW THAT JAMES HAD A LARGE NETWORK OF GANG FOR ATTACK. HE ALSO HAS SOME INTERNATIONAL CRIMINALS AND DANGEROUS ILLEGAL WEPONS. HE PERFECTLY PLANNED AND STARTED THE MISSON BY KILLING THE LEADER'S CHILDREN THEN MAKING THE GOVERNMENT LOOKS WEAK BY ADDING DRUG INTO THE FOOD, ATTACKING THE ARMY BASE AND THEN FINALLY KILLING THE LEADER TO BRING DOWN THE GOVERNMENT. TO STOP JAMESTRIC, THOMAS NEEDS TO ARREST HIM. SO, HE STARTED TO MOVE TO NORTH AMERICA.

AT JOSE MARTI AIRPORT, CUBA,

WHEN THOMAS WAS STANDING IN THE AIRPORT, HE SAW A MAN , HIDING HIS FACE WITH CAP AND CROSSING HIM. THOMAS FELT THAT THE FACE WAS FAMILIAR TO HIM. SO THOMAS FOLLOWED THE MAN AND FOUND THAT IT WAS PETER HUBER. PETER STARTED TO WALK FAST. THOMAS STARTED TO CHASE. THERE ROGER ENTERED AND CAUGHT PETER. THOMAS ARRESTED HIM AND GOT PETER TO POLICE STATION. THOMAS CANCELLED HIS FLIGHT TICKET. AT POLICE STATION, THOMAS TORTURED PETER TO GET THE TRUTH FROM HIM. THOMAS HIT PETER SEVERELY. NOT EVEN WATER WAS GIVEN TO HIM. HE WAS CONTINUOUSLY TORTURED FOR 3 HOURS. THEN THOMAS MADE A DEAL THAT HE WILL LEAVE PETER WITHOUT ANY CASE ON HIM IF HE

SAYS THE TRUTH. THOMAS GAVE WATER TO PETER AND ASKED ABOUT HIM AND RELATION WITH JAMES. PETER WANT ABLE TO WITHSTAND THE PAIN ANYMORE, SO HE STARTED TO SAY THE TRUTH.

PETER AND JAMES

WHEN KURK FAMILY WAS KILLED BY THE CUBAN PEOPLE, THESE TWO KIDS (JAMES AND ANNA) WERE LEFT IN THE STREETS OF CUBA LIKE ORPHANS. PETER HUBER WAS THE UNCLE OF JAMES. HE SEARCHED FOR ANNA AND JAMES FOR 2 WEEKS. AFTER A LONG SEARCH, HE FOUND THEM IN THE STREETS OF HAVANA. DUE TO THIS SITUATION, PETER, ANNA AND JAMES MOVED TO SWEDEN. THERE PETER AND JAMES WENT FOR WORK IN IRON MANUFACTURING INDUSTRY. BEFORE 2 YEARS THEY GOT THE NEWS THAT THE RULES ARE CHANGED IN GERMANY AND IT WAS FOR THE PEOPLE. SO THEY QUITTED THEIR JOB AND WENT TO GERMANY. THERE JAMES PLANNED TO TAKE REVENGE ON CUBAN PEOPLE. SO HE STARTED TO MAKE A HUGE PLAN AND STARTED ILLEGAL BUSINESSES. FROM THAT ILLEGAL BUSINESSES, HE GOT FRIENDS WHO ARE MOST WANTED CRIMINALS. HE GATHERED MANY OF THEM AND CREATED A UNION TO ATTACK CUBA. HE GOT MANY DANGEROUS WEAPONS FROM TERRORISTS. WITH THE HELP OF THOSE WEAPONS HE PLANNED TO DESTROY THE CUBAN ARMY BASE. AFTER HEARING THESE FROM PETER, THOMAS THANKED HIM FOR THE KIND INFORMATION, AND FINALLY... SHOT PETER. THEN, TO ARREST JAMES, THOMAS PLANNED TO MOVE TO NORTH AMERICA.

CHAPTER SIX

THE LOST COP

THE DAY NIGHT, AFTER THE ENQUIRY WITH PETER. THOMAS AND ROGER PLANNED THEIR TRAVEL TO NORTH AMERICA. THE FLIGHT TIMING FOR THEM WAS AT 8.00 AM. ROGER WOKE FROM HIS BED AT 7.30 AM. HE GOT READY QUICKLY AND ARRIVED TO AIRPORT AT 7.50 AM. BUT, THOMAS HAD NOT ARRIVED YET. ROGER TOOK HIS PHONE TO MAKE A CALL TO THOMAS. THERE HE FOUND THAT THOMAS ALREADY CALLED HIM 4 TIMES. ROGER MADE A CALL TO THOMAS. BUT THE PHONE WAS NOT REACHABLE. SO, HE WENT TO THE POLICE STATION. ROGER SEARCHED FOR THOMAS. BUT, HE WAS NOT FOUND ANYWHERE. THEN ROGER NOTICED THE TIMING OF MISSED CALLS MADE BY THOMAS. THE TIMINGS ARE 12.02 AM, 12.16 AM, 12.31 AM AND 12.36 AM. ROGER GAVE THESE INFORMATION TO CONTROL ROOM AND INSTRUCTED THEM TO LOCATE THE PHONE AT GIVEN TIME. THE CONTROL ROOM OFFICER SAID THAT THE PHONE WAS LOCATED IN HAVANA'S HIGHWAY AT 12.02 AM, THEN AT 12.16 AM THE PHONE WAS LOCATED IN AIRPORT AND AT 12.36 AM THE PHONE SIGNALWAS LOST. ROGER GUESSED SOMETHING IS WRONG. SO, HE GONE TO AIRPORT

FOR INVESTIGATION. AT AIRPORT, ROGER ASKED ABOUT THE FLIGHT DETAILS AROUND 12.45 AM TO 2.00 AM. THE AIRPORT FACULTY SAID THAT, 2 PLANES DEPARTED FROM CUBA. ONE IS A SPECIAL PLANE TO NORTH AMERICA AND OTHER IS TO GERMANY. THE NORTH AMERICA PLANE MOVED BY 1.00 AM AND THE GERMAN PLANE MOVED BY 1.15 AM. ROGER ENQUIRED ABOUT THOMAS SANCHER. THE FACULTY SAID THAT, THOMAS SANCHER BOOKED TICKETS IN BOTH THE PLANE. ROGER CONFUSED. THEN, ROGER HAD A CALL FROM CONTROL ROOM STATING THAT THOMAS PHONE AGAIN TRACKED BETWEEN 12.56 AM TO 1.05 AM. THEN ROGER GONE INTO THE AIRPORT CONTROL ROOM TO CHECK THE CAMERA. THERE HE SAW THOMAS WAS SITTING ALONE. AROUND 12.55 AM, A MAN CAME AND SPOKE WITH THOMAS. THEN, THOMAS SWITCHED ON HIS MOBILE AND MADE A CALL. SUDDENLY, THERE IS A POWERCUT AT AIRPORT. IN FRACTION OF SECOND GENERATER SWITCHED ON. BUT, CAMERA TOOK A MINUTE TO SWITCH ON. BETWEEN THIS SMALL INTERVAL OF A MINUTE, THOMAS AND THE UNKNOWN PERSON WENT MISSING. THEY WERE NOT CAUGHT IN ANY OF THE CAMERAS AROUND AIRPORT. ROGER REWINED THE FOOTAGE AND NOTICED THAT THE UNKNOWN MAN THAT SPOKE WITH THOMAS WAS RAUL CORRALES (SON OF ALBERTO KORDA). ROGER WAS SHOCKED BECAUSE HE HAD BEEN KILLED AND TIED ON THE POST AT THE GROUND. ROGER WAS CONFUSED AND ASKED THE RECEPTIONIST ABOUT THE AEROPLANE IN WHICH THOMAS TRAVELLED. SHE REPLIED THAT THE PLANE WAS GERMAN

SPACEAIR. ROGER INSTRUCTED THE CONTROL OFFICE TO TRACK THE CALL MADE BY THOMAS DURING 12.56 AM. OFFICERS IN CONTROL ROOM TRACKED AND SAID THAT THE CALL WAS MADE TO A TAXI DRIVER OF GERMANY. ROGER MADE A CALL TO ADOLF AND EXPLAINED ABOUT THE NEW PROBLEM. ADOLF ARRANGED A TEAM IN GERMANY TO SEARCH THOMAS. ADOLF MOVED TO THE GERMAN AIRPORT AND SAW THE CAMERA FOOTAGES. THERE HE SAW A TAXI DRIVER HAD A BOARD WITH THE NAME OF THOMAS AND A MAN MET THAT TAXI DRIVER. ADOLF ZOOMED THE FOOTAGE AND FOUND THAT THE MAN WAS NOT THOMAS AND SOMEONE USED HIS NAME. ADOLF TOOK A PHOTO OF THAT MAN AND SENT TO ROGER. ADOLF MADE A CALL TO ROGER AND ASKED ABOUT THE OTHER PERSON WHO SPOKE WITH THOMAS AT AIRPORT. ROGER SAID THAT, THE OTHER PERSON IS RAUL CORRALES WHO WAS REPORTED TO BE KILLED ALREADY. ADOLF ASKED THE PHOTO OF RAUL CORRALES. WHEN ADOLF SAW THE PHOTO, HE FELT THAT THE PERSON IN PHOTO WAS FAMILIAR TO HIM. ADOLF STARTED TO SEARCH HIS PHOTO IN ALL CASE FILES. THE PHOTO OF RAUL MATCHES THE PHOTO OF A PERSON IN HIS CASE WHO HAVE BEEN LOST BEFORE 2 MONTHS. ADOLF SAID THESE INFORMATION TO ROGER AND HE FOUND THAT THE DEAD PERSON WAS NOT RAUL CORRALES. NOW THE QUESTION WAS, WHERE WERE THOMAS AND RAUL CORRALES?.

AT CUBA,

ROGER WENT TO THE PRESIDENT'S OFFICE AND CONVEYED THE INFORMATION ABOUT THOMAS. FAIZON FELT BAD. FAIZON SAID THAT, THOMAS WAS THE ONLY PERSON WHO KNOWS ALL INFORMATION ABOUT THE CASE. FAIZON ASKED ROGER TO BRING THE CASE FILE OF JAMES. ROGER MADE A CALL TO A COP IN POLICE STATION AND ASKED HIM TO BRING THE CASE FILE. THE COP SEARCHED AND SAID THAT THE FILE WAS MISSING. FAIZON WAS FURIOUS. HE ORDERED TO SEARCH THOMAS ALL OVER THE COUNTRY. ROGER REQUESTED ADOLF TO SEARCH IN GERMANY.

AT GERMANY,

ADOLF WENT TO HOME OF THE PERSON WHO FILED THE CASE OF THAT MISSING MAN. ADOLF ENQUIRED THEM AND CAME TO KNOW THAT, JAMES AND THIS FAMILY HAS A MISUNDERSTANDING BEFORE SOME YEARS. SO, JAMES USED THIS OPPORTUNITY AND KIDNAPPED RAUL CORRALES. HE KILLED THE MISSING MAN AND PORTRAIED THAT RAUL CORRALES WAS DEAD. ADOLF CONVEYED THIS INFORMATION TO ROGER. ROGER CONVEYED THE MESSAGE TO FAIZON, FAIZON MADE ROGER AS THE HEAD OFFICER IN THE MISSION TO FIND THOMAS.

CHAPTER SEVEN

THE CRIMINAL COP

AT CUBA,

ALL COPS WERE ALERTED. ROGER FEARED THAT, WHAT WOULD HAPPEN IF THOMAS GOT CAUGHT BY JAMES. THEN ROGER HAD A CALL FROM ADOLF SEEKING THE PHONE NUMBER OF THE TAXI DRIVER. WHEN ADOLF GOT THE PHONE NUMBER, HE TRACKED AND FOUND ITS LOCATION.

AT GERMANY,

ADOLF ARRESTED THE TAXI DRIVER FOR ENQUIRY. DURING ENQUIRY, ADOLF ASKED ABOUT THE MAN WHO ARRIVED AT THE AIRPORT WITH THE NAME OF THOMAS SANCHER. TAXI DRIVER SAID THAT, HE DROPPED HIM AT THE HOTEL SACOVIANALL AND AFTER SOMETIME HE AGAIN TOOK THAT MAN TO AIRPORT. ADOLF GONE TO SACOVIANALL HOTEL AND INVESTIGATED ABOUT THAT MAN USING HIS IMAGE. THERE THE HOTEL RECEPTIONIST SAID THAT, THE NAME OF THAT MAN WAS LEVIN MAX. THEN ADOLF TRAVELLED TO AIRPORT FOR

INVESTIGATION. THERE HE CAME TO KNOW THAT, LEVIN MAX HAD AGAIN TRAVELLED TO CUBA. ADOLF SAID THIS INFORMATION TO ROGER. ROGER ALERTED THE POLICE FORCE AND ORDERED THEM TO FIND LEVIN MAX.

AT CUBA,

ROGER HAD GONE TO A COFFEE SHOP. THERE HE FOUND THAT A MAN INSIDE COFFEE SHOP HAD GUN IN HIS PANT POCKET. ROGER CLOSELY OBSERVED THAT MAN AND FOUND THAT, HE WAS LEVIN MAX. LEVIN PUSHED ROGER AND STARTED TO RUN. ROGER STARTED HIS CHASE. THEY WERE RUNNING BETWEEN THE SMALL STREETS OF HAVANA. SUDDENLY, A ROPE SLIPPED ROGER. A BIKE CROSSED HIM FASTLY AND PICKED UP LEVIN. THE MAN WHO DROVE THE BIKE WEARED A BLACK SUIT, BLACK SUNGLASS AND A BLACK SCARF.

IN NORTH AMERICA,

THE TERRORIST STARTED SETTING UP THE WEAPONS TO ATTACK CUBA. BUT, JAMES STOPPED THEM AND SAID THAT HE HAD A CALL FROM UNKNOWN PERSON STATING THAT THEY KIDNAPPED THOMAS AND THEY HAVE THE ILLEGAL INFORMATION OF OUR TERRORIST GANG WHICH IS BEING SEARCHED BY ALL COUNTRIES. THE TERRORIST GANG SAID THAT THE SPEAKER WAS FAKE. THEN JAMES DENIED AND REPLIED THAT THE SPEAKER WAS REAL BECAUSE THEY SHOWED THE EXACT LOCATION OF TERRORIST SPOT. THEN, JAMES

STARTED TO SEARCH THE UNKNOWN GANG AND THOMAS.

AT CUBA,

AFTER THE CHASE, ROGER WENT TO THE POLICE STATION. THERE HE GOT A LETTER WHICH INSISTED HIM TO MEET AT A CAFE. ROGER WENT THERE WITHOUT ANY PROTECTION. WHEN HE REACHED THE CAFE, HE SAW THOMAS, RAUL CORRALES AND LEVIN MAX. ROGER WAS TAKEN ABACK , HE QUESTIONED THOMAS ON HIS DRAMA. THEN THOMAS SAID THAT, HE GOT PHONE CALL FROM RAUL CORRALES ON THAT DAY WHICH SHOCKED HIM. RAUL SAID, HE NOTICED SOMEONE IN CUBAN POLICE DEPARTMENT IS WORKING FOR JAMES WHICH WAS OBSERVED BY HIM WHEN HE WAS KIDNAPPED. AO, THOMAS PLANNED TO EXECUTE HIS PLAN WITHOUT THE HELP OF CUBAN COPS. THOMAS ORDERED ROGER TO KEEP THE MESSAGE SECRET AND SAID HIM TO CONVEY THIS TO ADOLF.

THE CRIMINAL COP

AT NORTH AMERICA,

AGAIN JAMES HAD A CALL FROM THAT UNKNOWN PERSON. HE SAID JAMES TO OBEY HIS INFORMATION TO AVOID LOSING HIS TERRORIST GANG. JAMES WAS CONFUSED ABOUT THE CALLER. THE UNKNOWN PERSON WHO SPOKE WITH JAMES WAS LEVIN MAX. THIS WAS THE PLAN OF THOMAS SANCHER TO

CATCH JAMES. AS PER THOMAS PLAN, JAMES MADE A MISTAKE BY ARRIVING CUBA IN SEARCH OF THOMAS.

AT CUBA,

JAMES ARRIVED TO THE AIRPORT. HE BOOKED HIS ROOM NEAR AIRPORT.THOMAS SAID ROGER TO CLEAR THE POLICE FORCE NEAR AIRPORT TO AVOID HIS APPEARANCE TO POLICE AND TO TRACK JAMES. THOMAS, LEVIN AND ROGER MOVED TO THE HOTEL AND OPENED THE DOOR OF JAMES ROOM. THERE JAMES WAS MISSING AND THE CONTROL ROOM LOST THE CONNECTION OF JAMES THEY WENT BACK TO HOME WITH A HUGE DISAPPOINTMENT. WHEN THOMAS OPENED THE DOOR, HE SAW JAMES, SITTING ON THE CHAIR AND KEEPING RAUL CORRALES IN GUN POINT. THOMAS AND LEVIN FOCUSED THEIR GUN TOWARDS JAMES BUT, JAMES LAUGHED. BECAUSE, ROGER FOCUSED HIS GUN TOWARDS THOMAS AND LAUGHED.

NOW THOMAS SANCHER WAS LOCKED BY JAMES USING ROGER. THOMAS TOOK HIS PHONE AND MADE A TEXT "RELEASE THE EVIDENCES" AND SAID THAT, IF JAMES DONE ANYTHING WRONG THE MESSAGE WILL BE SENT TO THE POLICE TEAM. THOMAS ORDERED JAMES TO LEAVE RAUL CORRALES. JAMES HAD NO OPTION SO HE LEFT RAUL CORRALES. THOMAS SAID RAUL CORRALES TO OPEN THE DOOR. 20-25 POLICE ARRANGED BY THOMAS ARRIVED THERE AND ARRESTED JAMES AND ROGER. THOMAS STARTED HIS ENQUIRY WITH ROGER. FROM THAT ENQUIRY, THOMAS CAME TO KNOW THAT ROGER IS A GERMAN WHO CAME TO NORTH AMERICA IN

SEARCH OF BETTER LIFE. NORTH AMERICA HAD NOT PROVIDED THE EXPECTED LIFE TO HIM. SO HE CAME TO CUBA. THERE ROGER AND HIS FAMILY WAS ALSO ONE AMONG THOSE WHO WERE DISCRIMINATED. ROGER'S STORY WAS SAME AS OF JAMES. BUT, JAMES WENT TO SWEDEN WEREAS ROGER JOINED AS POLICE IN CUBA TO TAKE REVENGE. ROGER ASKED HOW THOMAS HAD FOUND THAT ROGER WAS INVLOVED IN THIS. THOMAS REPLIED THAT, WHEN RAUL CORRALES FIRST CALLED THOMAS, HE MENTIONED THAT A POLICE OFFICER IN CUBA IS AN INFORMER OF JAMES. THOMAS GUESSED IT AS ROGER BECAUSE, AT THAT TIME, ROGER WAS THE ONE WHO KNEW ALL THE INFORMATION AND PLAN MADE BY THOMAS. SO, THOMAS MADE MISSED CALLS TO DIVERT ROGER. THEN AGAIN THOMAS CAME IN FRONT OF ROGER TO CATCH JAMES. AS PER THE PLAN , HE USED ROGER AND MADE JAMES TO COME TO CUBA. NOW, THE WORK HAD BECOME EASIER. JAMES HAD BEEN ARRESTED. THESE PLAN OF THOMAS MADE JAMES FURIOUS .JAMES SAID THAT HIS GANG WILL DESTROY CUBA AS PER THE PLAN. THEY WILL NOT FOCUS ON THE RELEASE OF EVIDANCES. THEN THOMAS ASKED "WHICH EVIDANCES?". HE LAUGHED AND SAID THAT IT WAS THE DRAMA MADE BY HIM TO STOP THE ATTACK. THOMAS THOUGHT THE CASE WAS OVER. BUT, ON THE NEXT DAY, JAMES SAID THAT THE BOMBS ARE ARRIVING IN 3 HOURS AND STARTED TO LAUGH. THOMAS KICKED HIM AND ASKED "HOW?". JAMES SAID TO HIS GANG THAT, IF HE HAVE NOT ARRIVED IN A DAY THEN IMMEDIATELY THE ATTACK SHOULD BE STARTED. AFTER THIS INFORMATION, THOMAS TIGHTENED THE SECURITY

AND THE GOVERNMENT ORDERED LOCKDOWN FOR THE COUNTRY. WHOLE CUBA BECAME SILENT. SUDDENLY, A BIG BOMB BLAST WAS HEARD NEAR THE PORT. THERE A HUGE SHIP WITH FULL OF WEAPONS AND TERRORISTS ARRIVED INTO CUBA BY DAMAGING THE PORT SECURITY IN A SINGLE BOMB. THE CUBAN ARMY HEADED TOWARDS THE PORT. TERRORIST GANG HAD THE HUGE AMOUNT OF WEAPONS. CUBANS STARTED THEIR ATTACK. TERRORIST GANG CONTINUOUSLY THREW BOMBS ON CUBA FROM THE SHIP WHICH MADE THE CUBAN ARMY WEAKER. LARGE AMOUNT OF CUBAN SOILDERS HAD BEEN DEAD. THE DEFENSE WAS TOTALLY LOST. TERRORISTS STARTED TO MOVE INTO THE CITIES. EVERYONE THOUGHT THAT CUBA WILL BE DESTROYED. IF IT HAPPENS , IT WILL BE THE LARGEST TERRORIST ATTACK IN HISTORY. BUT, SUDDENLY A BOMB FROM SKY BLASTED THE SHIP OF THE TERRORISTS. ALL THE WEAPONS SINKED INSIDE THE WATER. THOMAS GOT A MESSAGE FROM ADOLF THAT, GERMAN ARMY WILL HELP CUBAN ARMY WITH PRESIDENT'S PERMISSION. THEN THE GERMAN ARMY STARTED THEIR ATTACK FROM THE AIR. PRESIDENT OF GERMANY HAD KEPT HIS PROMISE AND MADE IT REAL. CUBAN ARMY BEAT THE TERRORISTS WITH HELP OF GERMAN ARMY. AFTER A MONTH, JAMES, ROGER AND THE INTERNATIONAL TERRORIST GANG GOT DEATH SENTENCE. THE ENTIRE COUNTRY APPRECIATED THOMAS AND CUBA FOR DESTROYING THE MOST WANTED INTERNATIONAL TERRORISTS.

AFTER 2 YEARS,

RAUL CORRALES WAS ANNOUNCED AS THE NEW PRESIDENT. THOMAS WAS PROMOTED AS THE MOST POWERFUL OFFICIAL WHO HAS THE CONTROL OF ARMY AND POLICE.

Rise Of Terrorism

At North america,

Amith khan (The leader of terrorist) made a call to Thomas sancher stating that the attack on Cuba was not implemented for James and it was done for Thomas. Suddenly, Adolf spoke (He was in a conference call). Adolf asked "is everything is going fine" and he started to laugh jointly with Amith khan. Then, Thomas said,"Yes, Fine" and asked "is everything safe". Amith khan opened a room door. There, The Heisted materials of Cuban military weapons, Cuban Federal bank and Cuban Ornamental Museum are stored. The room is filled with weapons, gold, Money and costly materials. Thomas saw a news stating that, Cuba have been financially Attacked. Cuban Federal bank, Military weapons and Ornamental museum have been lost in fire. Thomas started to laugh, because the plan for the heist was made by Thomas. Thomas made Adolf to fire from the air which was not done for terrorists, The fire/bomb is implemented to damage the heisted buildings to clear the evidances and to spread the fake news. Adolf said that without Thomas Sancher, The heist is impossible and also said Thanks to Thomas. Amith khan said that the plan made by Thomas was great and extraordinary with his execution. Then, Thomas asked, where should he come for collecting his share. Amith khan said Adolf and Thomas to meet him at "IRAQ".

(The Lost Cop : Chapter-6, it is the time when Thomas and Adolf made a decision to stand with terrorists. Thomas made himself lost to plan the heist. He used the situation and James as the key for his heist. The need, plan and execution of Thomas Sancher's Heist will be explained).

****** The CRIMINALCop ******

Printed by Libri Plureos GmbH in Hamburg,
Germany